When a tramp asks an old woman for food, she declares indignantly that she hasn't a scrap in the house, that she hasn't had a bite to eat all day. Whereupon the tramp offers to make soup for both of them—from a nail. And so he does, with the aid of a few choice ingredients from the old woman's stores.

A Swedish Folk Tale

NAIL SOUP

Retold by Harve Zemach

Illustrated by Margot Zemach

Follett Publishing Company • Chicago

Library of Congress Catalog Card Number: 64-15635

123456789

NAIL SOUP

Once upon a time a tramp was making his way through a forest. He had not seen a house for many an hour, and he wondered where he might find shelter for the night. He thought to himself how nice it would be to warm up in front of a fire, and to have some dinner. But the sun was sinking, and there wasn't a cottage in sight.

Just then he met an old woman out gathering branches and twigs for kindling.

"Hello and good evening!" said the tramp, glad
as he could be to see her.

"Good evening," said the woman. "Where are you from?"

"Here and there, far and near," said the tramp. "I've seen the world, and I'm on my way home."

"Is that so?" said the woman. "And what is it you want hereabouts?"

"Well, I could use a place to stay for the night," he said.

"Just as I thought!" said the woman. "You had better keep on going, for my house is not an inn."

"My dear woman," said the tramp, "it is shameful to be so hardhearted and cross. We human beings are supposed to help each other when we can."

"Help each other? There's a good joke. Who do you suppose will help me? I haven't even got a scrap in the house! No, you'd better be on your way," she said.

But the tramp did not give up so easily. The old woman kept on complaining about her own troubles, and the tramp kept on urging and arguing, until at last she said all right, he could sleep on the floor if he wanted to.

He thanked her for her kindness.

"Rather be warm on the hard floor, than shiver and freeze outside the door," said he. This tramp had a quick wit and was always ready with a rhyme.

As soon as he got inside the house, he could tell that the woman was not as poor as she pretended to be, only stingy and greedy.

So he asked her in his most polite and pleasant manner for something to eat.

"How do you think I can feed you, when I haven't had a bite of food myself all day long?" said the woman.

But the tramp knew better.

He said: "Nothing all day long? Poor old granny, you must be starving! Better lend me a pot, then, and I shall make dinner for both of us."

"You'll make dinner!" said the woman. "How will you make dinner if there isn't any food?"

"Leave it to me," said the tramp. "I've learned things on my travels that most people have never even heard of."

The old woman wondered what it was all about, so she let him have a pot.

He poured in some water, put it on the fire, and blew with all his might to get the flame going strong.

Then he took from his pocket an ordinary nail, set it on the palm of his hand, turned it around three times, and dropped it into the pot.

The woman watched the nail sink down to the bottom.

"What's this going to be?" she asked.

"Nail soup," said the tramp, and he began stirring the water with a stick.

"Nail soup?" asked the woman.

"That's right, nail soup," said the tramp.

The old woman thought she had seen and heard just about everything in her time, but making soup with a nail—well, that was something new!

"If you want to learn how to make it," said the tramp, "just watch me. Then you won't ever again have to go all day without a bite."

He went on stirring the soup, and she watched as hard as she could.

"You know," he said, "I have been making soup with this same nail for over a week, so our soup may be rather thin. Of course, if one had a speck of flour or sifted oatmeal to add to it, then we could be sure of a good meal. But," he said, "we'll have to do without it, and not think twice about it." And he kept on stirring the soup.

"Wait, I might have some flour somewhere,"
said the old woman. She went to fetch it, and it was
the finest sort.

The tramp sprinkled the flour into the soup and kept on stirring, while the woman stared first at him and then at the pot and then back at him again.

"It's coming along," he said. "It's almost good enough to serve for company. Add a few potatoes and a bit of salted beef, and it would be a dish fit for gentlefolks," he said. "But we'll have to do without it, and not think twice about it."

The old woman thought for a while, and then she remembered where she might find some potatoes, and even a bit of beef. She got them and gave them to the tramp, and he kept on stirring.

"This will be a grand soup," he said. "It's not everyone that gets to taste such a grand soup as this!"

"You don't say!" said the woman. "Is that so! And just imagine—all from a nail!"

"All it lacks now is a little barley and a drop of milk. Then we could invite the king to have some, if we wanted to," said the tramp. "This is what the king himself eats every evening—the king's cook told me so."

"Dear me! The king himself!" cried the woman, slapping her knees.

"But we'll have to do without it, and not think twice about it," said the tramp.

The woman went to look, and sure enough, she did have some barley; and there was also milk, as much as was needed.

The tramp stirred and stirred and stirred.

Then suddenly he stopped and fished out the nail from the steaming kettle.

"It is ready," he said. "Now we'll have a feast, just like the king and queen. Except, of course, when *they* eat this kind of soup, they always have a sandwich with it, and wine. And a tablecloth on the table. But we'll have to do without it, and not think twice about it."

Well, by this time the old woman was beginning to feel like quite a grand lady. She thought that if the king and queen had it that way, then she and the tramp might as well have it the same. She hurried to the cupboard and got out the wine bottle, glasses, cheese, butter, smoked beef and veal. The table could hardly hold it all.

Never in that old woman's life had she had such
a good time, and never had she tasted such rich soup
—and to think that it was all from a nail!

They ate and they drank and they danced around
the room, and then they ate and drank some more.

And when they finally got sleepy, and the tramp was going to lie down on the floor, the old woman said: "No, no! Such a person must have a bed to lie in."

"It's just like the sweet Christmas," said the tramp. "In all my travels I have never met a nicer woman." And he lay down on the bed and fell fast asleep.

When he got up the next morning, the old woman gave him coffee and a bun. And before he said good-bye, she handed him a bright silver piece.

"And thank you for teaching me how to make soup with a nail," she said, "because now that I know how, I shall always live in comfort."

"That's all right," said the tramp. "It's easy if you remember to add something good to it."

Then the tramp went on his way, and the old woman stood at the door, watching him go.

"Such people don't grow on trees," she said.